A CODE QUEST ADVENTURE

TITANIC

Written by Anita Croy

Illustrated by Mick Posen

KINGFISHER
LONDON & NEW YORK

Copyright © Kingfisher 2012
Published in the United States by Kingfisher,
175 Fifth Ave., New York, NY 10010
Kingfisher is an imprint of Macmillan Children's Books, London.
All rights reserved.

Created for Kingfisher by Brown Bear Books Ltd.
Original concept: Jo Connor
Narrative concept: Simon Holland

Distributed in the U.S. and Canada by Macmillan,
175 Fifth Ave., New York, NY 10010

Library of Congress Cataloging-in-Publication data
has been applied for.

ISBN: 978-0-7534-6672-8

Kingfisher books are available for special promotions and
premiums. For details contact: Special Markets Department,
Macmillan, 175 Fifth Ave., New York, NY 10010.

For more information, please visit www.kingfisherbooks.com

Printed in China
1 3 5 7 9 8 6 4 2
1TR/1211/LFG/UNTD/200MA

CONTENTS

Hi, I'm Brendan. I'm a reporter on a newspaper in Liverpool, England, and I need your help to piece together my latest news story.

MEET BRENDAN

Who are the mysterious children who are also on the voyage?

April 27, 2012

Dear Code Breaker,

One day I came into the office to find my editor waiting for me. He handed me a ticket for a voyage to mark the 100th anniversary of the sinking of the Titanic. He said that this would be my next writing assignment, if I wanted it. I jumped at the chance! The ship was registered in Liverpool, my hometown, and I've always been fascinated by the story.

My grandparents always said that we had a relative who was an engineer on the Titanic. My voyage would give me a chance to find out about him. It turned out to be a remarkable story.

Along the way, I had to break many coded messages and puzzles. I made sure to write them all down. Now you will have a chance to solve them yourself in this book.

Good luck!

Here is your challenge: read my story and look at all the clues and evidence I found. Can you break the codes, figure out the puzzles, and solve the mystery along with me?

TRAGIC VOYAGE
The *Titanic* struck an iceberg and sank on its first-ever voyage in 1912. Of the 2,223 people onboard, more than 1,500 died.

The clues could be anywhere. Look out for the evidence in each exciting scene.

HOW TO USE THIS BOOK

As you read through the book, you will see exciting scenes from my adventure. These are followed by "code breaker" pages, in which I set out all of the clues for you to study. Evidence panels will show you the key codes in the story and tell you what you need to do to crack them. It is a good idea to make sure you have your compass code wheel nearby! Some paper and a pencil might be useful, too.

CODED DIRECTIONS

On many of the code-breaker spreads, you'll see a series of compass directions similar to the sample above. You'll need to align the compass wheel correctly to discover the words they stand for.

MISSING WORDS

As you decode the compass symbols, you may need to fill in verbs (action words) and other words to make sentences. Use your common sense!

THE CHARTS

Look out for foldout charts that summarize the information you need to break the codes.

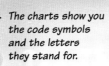

CODE BREAKER

COMMUNICATING IN DOTS AND DASHES
A skilled radio operator could send nearly 40 words per minute. Incoming signals were listened to on headphones and written down as words. The operators then typed up the completed message on a telegraph form.

The charts show you the code symbols and the letters they stand for.

HOW TO SET YOUR COMPASS WHEEL

My family had an old compass that they said belonged to our relative on the *Titanic*. I took it with me to follow the direction of my voyage.

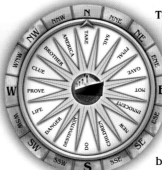

To set your compass wheel, you should figure out the direction of each stage of my voyage. Turn the inner ring of the compass so that the arrow points in that direction. The code words should now be in the right place.

SET YOUR COMPASS

On the pages with compass codes, you will find a map that shows the current stage of the voyage. Use the direction between the two points (shown in red), not the actual path of the ship.

SOLUTIONS

If you get stuck on a task, take a look at page 48, where all the answers are given and explained. But no cheating! The harder you try to solve the codes yourself, the better you will get and the more you will learn about the *Titanic*'s voyage.

The *Titanic* disaster ended a golden age of shipping. Companies competed to offer passengers the quickest and most comfortable trip across the Atlantic.

OCEAN CROSSINGS

BRUNEL'S BREAKTHROUGH

In 1837, British engineer Isambard Kingdom Brunel designed the S.S. *Great Western* to carry passengers across the Atlantic. The paddle-wheel steamship cut the journey time in half, from a month to just 15 days. Brunel's vessel started a new era. The race was on. Shipping lines raced to complete the voyage more and more quickly. Passengers began to cross the Atlantic in record numbers.

White Star had offices in Liverpool and London, England, and in New York City.

White Star Line

"OLYMPIC" & "TITANIC"

LARGEST STEAMERS IN THE WORLD

THE WHITE STAR LINE

The White Star Line, which owned the *Titanic*, was founded in 1871. It competed with its main rival, Cunard, for passengers. In the early 1900s, White Star chairman J. Bruce Ismay set out to build a fleet of luxury liners, including the *Titanic* and its sister ship, the *Olympic*. Ismay was onboard for the *Titanic's* fateful first voyage.

THE QUEST FOR SPEED

Shipping companies all wanted to claim the fastest crossing of the Atlantic. The title became known as the Blue Riband. In the 1890s, German liners were the fastest, but in 1909 Cunard took the Blue Riband with the *Mauretania*. Some people claimed that J. Bruce Ismay made the *Titanic* sail dangerously fast to try to claim the title for White Star. Below, some holders of the Blue Riband are listed with their average speed on the Atlantic crossing.

In the 1930s, this Blue Riband trophy was created.

1838: *Sirius*
United Kingdom
8.03 knots
(9.24 mph, or 14.87km/h)

1872: *Adriatic*
United Kingdom
14.65 knots
(16.86 mph, or 27.13km/h)

1885: *Etruria*
United Kingdom
19.56 knots
(22.51 mph, or 36.23km/h)

1909: *Mauretania*
United Kingdom
26.06 knots
(29.99 mph, or 48.26km/h)

A FIRST-CLASS PASSENGER LIST

The *Titanic*'s first-class passengers included some of the most famous people of the time. Businessman John Jacob Astor came from one of the United States' richest families. Benjamin Guggenheim had made millions from industry. Isidor Straus owned Macy's department store in New York City, and the British aristocrat Lady Duff Gordon was a famous fashion designer.

Benjamin Guggenheim
(died)

WHO WAS ONBOARD?

First class—329
(including 7 children)

Second class—285
(including 25 children)

Third class—710
(including 80 children)

Crew—899

Total—2,223

Isidor Straus
(died)

Lady Duff Gordon
(survived)

LOOKING FOR A NEW LIFE

Many third-class passengers onboard came from poor countries such as Ireland, Sweden, and even Syria, in the Middle East. They were among hundreds of thousands of immigrants who moved to the United States between 1880 and 1920 in the hope of finding a better life.

An Italian family lands in New York City in 1905. About 750,000 immigrants arrived each year, mainly from Europe.

The story of the *Titanic* has fascinated people for more than a century. The most famous steamship of its age sank on its very first voyage.

FATEFUL VOYAGE

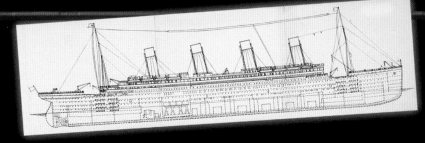

1 BELFAST
March 31, 1909 *Construction begins in Belfast, Ireland.*
May 31, 1911 *Titanic is launched.*
March 31, 1912 *Interior work on Titanic ends.*
April 2, 1912 *Titanic's sea trials.*

2 SOUTHAMPTON
April 10, 1912 *Titanic begins its first voyage.*

3 CHERBOURG
April 10, 1912 *Titanic picks up European passengers.*

4 QUEENSTOWN
April 11, 1912 *Titanic leaves Queenstown (Cobh), Ireland.*

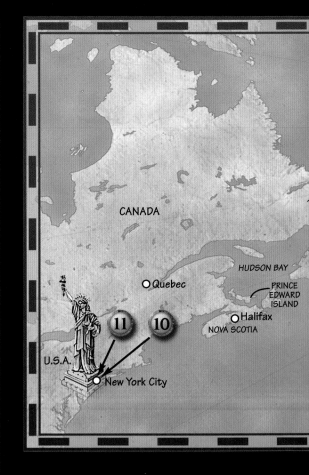

CANADA

HUDSON BAY

Quebec

PRINCE EDWARD ISLAND

11 10

Halifax
NOVA SCOTIA

U.S.A.

New York City

5 ATLANTIC
April 13, 1912 *Titanic* is warned of ice by a passing ship.

6 ICEBERG
April 14, 1912
11:40 P.M. *Titanic* strikes an iceberg; the front five compartments take on water.

7 SINKING
April 15, 1912
12:05 A.M. *Titanic* begins to send distress signals.
12:45 A.M. The first lifeboats are lowered.
1:15 A.M. *Titanic*'s stern (back half) lifts out of the water.
2:05 A.M. The last lifeboat is lowered.

2:17 A.M. Last signal from the wireless room.
2:18 A.M. All the lights go out; the ship breaks in two. The front half sinks.
2:20 A.M. The stern half sinks.

9 RESCUE
4:10 A.M. *Carpathia* begins to pick up survivors.
8:50 A.M. *Carpathia* heads for New York.

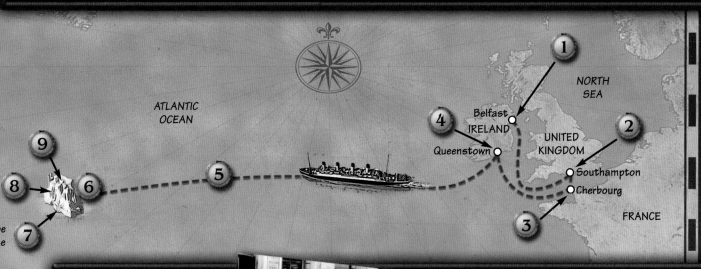

NORTH SEA

ATLANTIC OCEAN

Belfast
IRELAND

Queenstown

UNITED KINGDOM

Southampton

Cherbourg

FRANCE

10 RELATIVES
April 15, 1912
Anxious relatives gather at the White Star Line offices in New York City.

11 SURVIVORS
April 18, 1912
The *Carpathia* reaches New York City with survivors.

ENGINE-ROOM HEROES

By the wharf in Liverpool, England, is a monument to the 244 engineers who died on the *Titanic*. Some were from Liverpool, where the White Star Line had its headquarters.

I saw that a young boy and girl were already there. They wore old-fashioned raincoats. When they saw me, they ran away.

While I was wondering what had scared them, I tripped over something. It was an old suitcase. The children must have left it. What should I do? I thought something inside the suitcase might tell me who they were so I could give it back to them.

When I opened the suitcase, I was disappointed. It was just full of old paper. But then I saw that it was all about the *Titanic*. There was so much information: newspapers, letters, postcards, pictures . . .

I decided to take the suitcase with me on my trip. I was fascinated to look through its contents. Someone had collected every scrap of information about the ship.

CLUES IN THE CASE

I couldn't leave the suitcase in the rain. The contents would have been ruined if they had gotten wet. It was better to take it with me and try to return it to its owners later.

The suitcase might also contain clues about how I could return it to its owners. As we sailed to Belfast, I studied the papers. The oldest was an envelope labeled "March 1912"—the month before the *Titanic* sailed.

SHIPBUILDING CITY
In the early 20th century, the Harland and Wolff shipyard was the biggest employer in Belfast. The hulls of the ships towered over the terraced streets where the workers lived.

CODE ONE: NEWS HEADLINES

The envelope held two sheets of paper and many tiny pieces that looked as if they had been cut out of newspapers. Can you put the words together to figure out the headlines?

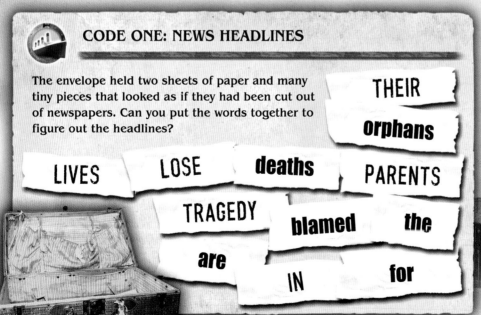

THEIR

orphans

LIVES   LOSE   deaths   PARENTS

TRAGEDY   blamed   the

are

IN   for

It seemed to me as though the envelope and its contents were older than the rest of the stuff in the suitcase. March 1912 was the month before the *Titanic* sailed. Perhaps these clues related to someone who was on that original voyage.

ENGINEERS' MONUMENT

There are many monuments to the *Titanic* and its crew. The monument in Liverpool honors the engineers, who stayed at their posts to keep the ship afloat for as long as possible.

The suitcase held newspapers, photos, letters, sheets of music, and even an old key.

CODE TWO: THE NUMBER CODE

The envelope also contained a larger piece of paper. It was mostly covered in numbers, and some had clues next to them. Whoever had made these notes did not want them to be easy to understand. But perhaps the questions were a key to the rest of the writing.

Can you answer the questions (below) and use the answers to figure out which letter each number stands for in the code? It might help if you write out the alphabet and note each number next to the appropriate letter.

Capital of France 6 11 7 25 26

Where Titanic was built 20 19 13 2 11 26 8

Titanic's destination 5 19 10 22 17 7 3

Titanic's captain 26 4 25 8 18

Using the code-breaker alphabet you have made, can you decipher the remaining words on the paper? They may relate to information about the original voyage.

26 19 11 5 =   4 19 24 11 5 =

26 8 17 10 11 10 11 22 26 =

19 5 24 25 5 19   7 17 17 4 =

26 8 17 7 19 7 17 17 4 =

SET YOUR COMPASS

To set your compass wheel, you should figure out the direction of this part of my journey, from Liverpool to Belfast.

CODE THREE: FMcD'S MESSAGE

The third piece of paper in the envelope contained only what looked like some compass directions and some initials, "FMcD." Can you use your compass wheel to decipher the meaning of the directions?

NW

ESE

E

SSW

The *Titanic* was not only the largest and most luxurious ocean liner ever built. It was also intended to be the safest.

UNSINKABLE SHIP

THOMAS ANDREWS

Engineer Thomas Andrews sailed on the *Titanic* to check that everything went well on its first voyage. He believed that the ship was almost perfect. After the collision, however, he realized that the ship would sink quickly.

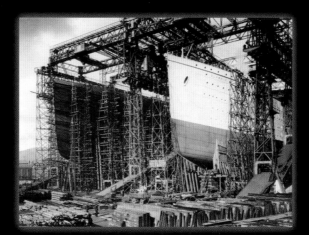

CONSTRUCTION OF THE SHIP

Construction of the *Titanic* began in March 1909 at the Harland and Wolff shipyard in Belfast. About 11,300 men worked on the ship and its sister ship, the *Olympic*. The huge ships towered over the city. The steel hull plates each measured 33 ft. (10m) across. It took three million rivets to hold them in place.

More than 100,000 people saw the *Titanic*'s launch in Belfast.

Launch
of White Star Royal Mail Triple-Screw Steamer
"TITANIC"
At BELFAST.
Wednesday, 31st May, 1911, at 12-15 p.m.
Admit Bearer.

LAUNCHED!

The *Titanic* was launched on May 31, 1911. It took another year to construct and decorate the interior to luxurious standards. On April 2, 1912, the ship was tested for seaworthiness. It passed all the tests. The *Titanic* was ready to sail.

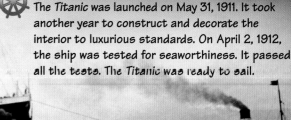

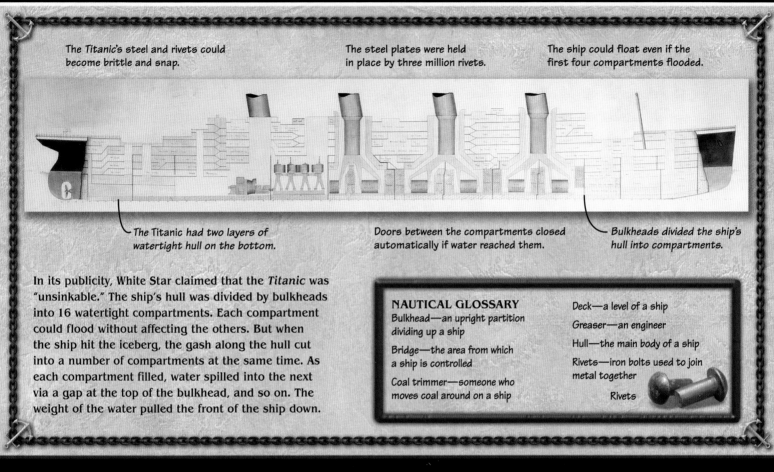

The *Titanic*'s steel and rivets could become brittle and snap.

The steel plates were held in place by three million rivets.

The ship could float even if the first four compartments flooded.

The Titanic had two layers of watertight hull on the bottom.

Doors between the compartments closed automatically if water reached them.

Bulkheads divided the ship's hull into compartments.

In its publicity, White Star claimed that the *Titanic* was "unsinkable." The ship's hull was divided by bulkheads into 16 watertight compartments. Each compartment could flood without affecting the others. But when the ship hit the iceberg, the gash along the hull cut into a number of compartments at the same time. As each compartment filled, water spilled into the next via a gap at the top of the bulkhead, and so on. The weight of the water pulled the front of the ship down.

NAUTICAL GLOSSARY

Bulkhead—an upright partition dividing up a ship

Bridge—the area from which a ship is controlled

Coal trimmer—someone who moves coal around on a ship

Deck—a level of a ship

Greaser—an engineer

Hull—the main body of a ship

Rivets—iron bolts used to join metal together

Rivets

THE CREW

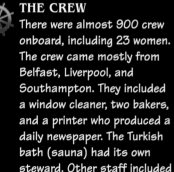

There were almost 900 crew onboard, including 23 women. The crew came mostly from Belfast, Liverpool, and Southampton. They included a window cleaner, two bakers, and a printer who produced a daily newspaper. The Turkish bath (sauna) had its own steward. Other staff included French and Italian waiters who worked in the Café Parisien.

Of the ship's eight officers, only four survived the disaster (marked with the * symbol).

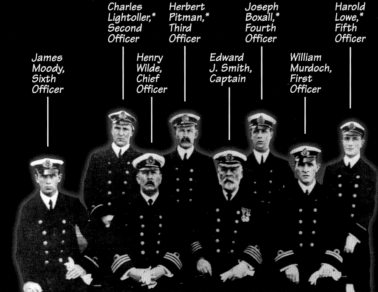

James Moody, Sixth Officer

Charles Lightoller,* Second Officer

Henry Wilde, Chief Officer

Herbert Pitman,* Third Officer

Edward J. Smith, Captain

Joseph Boxall,* Fourth Officer

William Murdoch, First Officer

Harold Lowe,* Fifth Officer

SOME OF THE *TITANIC*'S CREW AND THEIR JOBS

Officers (left)—8
Deck crew—59
Firemen (stokers)—176
Coal trimmers—73
Greasers—33
Mess hall stewards—6
Stewards and stewardesses—343
Galley staff—62
Restaurant staff—69
Postal clerks—5
Guarantee group—9
Musicians—8

MEMORIAL VOYAGE

To begin the memorial voyage, I had to go to Belfast, where the *Titanic* was built. I went straight to the site of a new museum being built over the slipways where the *Titanic* and the *Olympic* were constructed. The builders' scaffolding made it easy to imagine how these enormous ships once rose up like giants above the city.

Some large pieces of iron still lay on the slipway. They looked like they might have been parts of ships. I was studying them when I heard some metal fall to the floor with a loud *CLANG!* behind me. What was that? I had thought I was alone. I ran toward where the sound had come from. As I got there, I thought I saw two figures disappearing into the distance.

But someone had been drawing on an iron girder. There was a big white chalk circle with symbols inside it. What were they?

It was obvious that where I was standing had once been part of the shipyard. Maybe this was one of the slipways where the *Titanic* was built.

GHOSTLY MESSAGE

Someone had marked the girders only recently. The chalk looked fresh. It circled what looked like letters scratched into the metal. They were very worn and hard to read.

The iron girders lying around looked as if they had not been moved for decades.

CODE FOUR: A GIRDER

The girder looked as if it must have been there for many years. The writing was old, too. Can you decipher the words?

WH T AB T TE R VTS

ART HR NGH LFBATS

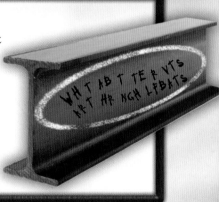

SET YOUR COMPASS

For the codes on these pages, the compass wheel needs to be set for the *Titanic*'s journey from Belfast to Southampton.

CODE FIVE: THE COMPASS

I had taken a ticket from the suitcase for the *Titanic*'s launch—perhaps from this very dock. Now I saw that it had some compass directions on the back. Another code!

 N

 NW

 SW

 SSE

Ticket to the launch of the *Titanic*.

Launch
OF
White Star Royal Mail Triple-Screw Steamer
"TITANIC"
At BELFAST,
Wednesday, 31st May, 1911, at 12-15 p.m.
Admit Bearer.

CODE SIX: THE MAZE

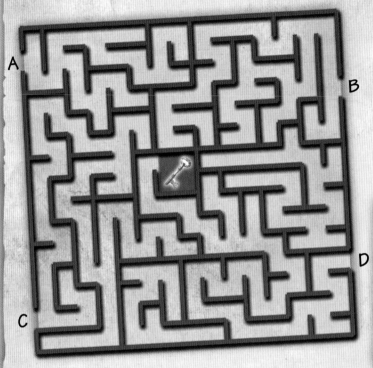

A

B

C

D

One plan did not look like the others. I realized that this was not an official diagram. It was more like a map . . . or a maze. Someone must have drawn it with the intention of providing directions to a particular part of the ship. But who were the directions for?

The ship was a maze of cabins, galleys, storerooms, and holds. The engine rooms were on the lowest decks.

Funnels released smoke from the boilers.

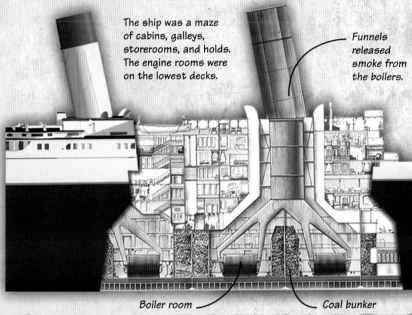

Boiler room

Coal bunker

I was excited to find the messages on the girder. But, as we sailed from Belfast, I went back through the suitcase to find out more about how the *Titanic* was built. Somewhere among the documents, I thought I had seen something that looked like plans.

NINE DECKS

The nine decks of the *Titanic* were full of corridors, cabins, storerooms, and other rooms. The first-class cabins were on the top three decks, with the second- and third-class areas below them. The lower decks housed cargo holds and the engines and furnaces.

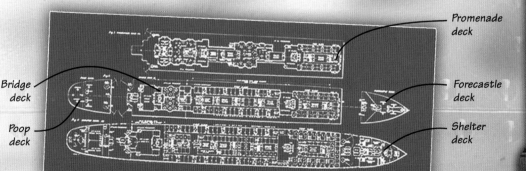

Promenade deck

Bridge deck

Poop deck

Forecastle deck

Shelter deck

PLACE OF DEPARTURE

From Belfast, we sailed to Southampton. Most passengers boarded the *Titanic* there. Most of the crew came from there, too. The local museum had an exhibition for the 100th anniversary. There were several artifacts salvaged from the ship, and even a reconstruction of the grand staircase from the first-class section.

One display had a lot of pictures of the passengers and crew. As I studied it, I saw the name Frank McDowell, who worked in the engine room. That was him: "FMcD"! He had a strange smile. I wondered what his secret might be.

But the label beneath the photograph said that Frank had drowned. I looked for the names "Sean" and "Megan"—but found neither. I began to wonder if they were even on the ship. Who could they have been?

LIFE ON DECK

The promenade decks had been designed to leave plenty of room for strolling, sitting, or playing games. The weather was cold, so passengers who went outside had to bundle up.

There was plenty of room outside for passengers to promenade, or take walks.

Six-year-old Robert Spedden spins a top on the promenade deck.

PASSING THE TIME

For active passengers, there was a gymnasium, a swimming pool, and a squash court, as well as a Turkish bath (a type of sauna). Others preferred going to the barber, playing billiards, or visiting the Café Parisien. In third class, passengers played cards or enjoyed sing-alongs.

Cards and billiards were some of the games played to pass the time on the long voyage.

There were separate lending libraries and reading rooms for first- and second-class passengers.

THE EMPTY WHARF

We sailed to Cherbourg, France, where the *Titanic* picked up 274 passengers, and on to the last stop, Queenstown, Ireland. The port, which is now called Cobh (pronounced "Cove"), is a sleepy place, but all the big liners used to dock here. You can still see the old gangways.

As I stood on the wharf, a shiver ran through me. I turned and saw a man watching me. His collar was turned up, and his hat was pulled down over his eyes, so I couldn't see his face.

As I walked through the empty streets, I thought I saw the man again. There was something about the way the shadows played on his clothes. At times it looked as if you could see right through him.

I got the feeling that there were other ghosts rushing past, as if the quiet harbor was once again the center of activity.

The harbor at Cobh was full of ghosts of the past. I stood on the old wooden jetty and imagined watching the *Titanic* steam out of sight over the horizon.

THE ENVELOPE

The envelope held more pieces of old paper and an old key. But there was a letter, too, and it had today's date on it.

There was a tug on my sleeve. A young boy held out an envelope. "The man asked me to give you this," he said.
"What man?" I asked.
"Over there." The boy pointed . . . but the wharf was empty.

 PORT OF DEPARTURE
Between 1850 and 1950, about 2.5 million Irish emigrants sailed from Cobh to a new life in the United States. In 1912, 123 passengers boarded the *Titanic* at Cobh.

 CODE NINE: THE COMPASS

It sounds strange, but the letter in the envelope felt as if it was intended for me. But I did not understand. What story was I supposed to tell? The first of the clues I took out of the envelope used the familiar code. Can you use the code wheel to decipher it?

 WAITING ROOMS
The White Star Line had an office on the wharf at Cobh. There was a special waiting room for first-class passengers. Third-class passengers waited outside.

 SET YOUR COMPASS

Set your compass wheel to the direction from Cherbourg to Queenstown to solve the code on this page.

N

SW

ESE   ENE

Tuesday, April 10

TO WHOM IT MAY CONCERN,
You must tell our story to the world.
All the clues you need are in the
suitcase. They will tell a tale of a
brave man and of two innocent
people who were falsely accused.

LUNCHEON

CON(S)OMMÉ FERMIER

COCKIE L(EE)KIE SOUP

FILLETS OF BRILL

EGG À L'(AR)GENTEUIL

CORNED BEEF,

VEGETABLES, DU(M)PLINGS

CHIC(K)EN À LA MARYLAND

(G)RILLED MUTTON CHOPS

MASHED, FRIED, & B(A)KED

POTATO(E)S

APPLE MERI(N)GUE

BUFFET

SA(L)MON MAYONNAIS(E)

POTTED SHRIMP

(N)ORWEGIAN ANCHOVIES

SOUSED HERRI(N)GS

PLAIN & SMOKED

(S)ARDINES

ROAST BEEF

RO(U)ND OF (S)PICED BEEF

VEAL & H(A)M PIE

VIRGI(N)IA &

CUMBERLAND HAM

CODE TEN: MENU CARDS

There were two menus from the first-class dining room. Some letters had been circled on each card. Can you spell out two names from the first card? And two more from the second? Perhaps the stowaways had changed their names . . . ?

Titanic china salvaged from the wreck

Original bottle and glasses

The *Titanic* was in Cobh for only a couple of hours, but the port became famous as the ship's final port of call. It gave me chills to think of those passengers taking their last steps on dry land.

LUCKY ESCAPE

It is said that a man from Cobh worked in the *Titanic*'s engine room. In his home port, he decided to jump ship. He hid under a tarpaulin on a boat heading to shore. No one knows if the story is true—but if it is, it was a lucky escape.

CODE ELEVEN: PICK THE LOCK

I was learning more about the mysterious stowaways. The final item in the envelope was an old key. I was sure it came from the ship. Can you use your judgment to figure out which door the key opened? This might reveal the place where the stowaways managed to hide onboard without being discovered.

Engine room

Radio room

Kitchen

Storeroom

Library

Gymnasium

THE CEREMONY

There was a ceremony late at night to mark the very spot where the *Titanic* sank, but I had fallen asleep. I was woken up by music and rushed up on deck. It was empty. Oh no! I must have slept through the ceremony.

Just then, two small figures appeared from the shadows and approached the railings. They threw something overboard. It was a wreath. I was sure I recognized the boy and girl from Liverpool. I called out, but they stepped back into the shadows.

I ran to the spot where they had disappeared—and bumped into a sailor. "Where did the children go?" I asked him. "Who?" he said. "There's nobody else here. I'm getting ready for the ceremony." "But hasn't it already happened? Isn't that why the band was playing music?" "What band? What music? Are you sure you're feeling all right, sir?"

FMcD

NNWSWNNWSE

I was lucky to find Frank's grave. Only 121 of the 1,517 victims are buried in the Fairview Lawn Cemetery in Halifax, Canada. A third of them were never identified.

TOMB CLUES

I noticed that someone had written something at the base of the gravestone. It was another compass code.

In all, only 328 bodies were found following the disaster. After being in the freezing water, most could not be identified. Many of them were reburied at sea. Fairview Lawn Cemetery is the resting place of the largest number of the *Titanic*'s victims.

SET YOUR COMPASS
For this clue, the compass wheel should be set to the direction of the *Titanic*'s unfinished journey, which would have taken it from Queenstown to New York City.

ATLANTIC OCEAN

DISCOVERED
The wreck of the *Titanic* was discovered in 1985. The ship lies on the seabed in two pieces, 2.5 mi. (4km) beneath the ocean's surface.

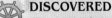

CODE FIFTEEN: GRAVE CODE
The message was smudged. As before, you'll need to set your compass wheel to read the code.

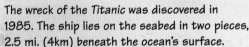

NNW   SW   NNW   SE

The 705 survivors picked up by the Carpathia landed in New York City three days later. There were official inquiries into the disaster in the United States and the United Kingdom. Among their other conclusions, they both judged that the Titanic had been sailing too quickly in an area where there were known to be icebergs.

As I studied Frank's grave, I suddenly realized something. Whoever the two children were, they were not among the victims. Perhaps they had safely reached the end of their journey.

The death toll of the disaster is thought to be 1,517—but people disagree about the exact number of victims.

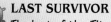
LAST SURVIVOR
The last of the *Titanic's* survivors, Millvina Dean, died in 2009—97 years after the disaster. She was a baby only a few weeks old when the ship sank and could not remember anything about it.

 ## CODE SIXTEEN: WORD FINDER

A piece of paper in the suitcase had a grid of letters. It included words that related to the story of the *Titanic*. Can you find all of the words to the right? They can go up, down, sideways, diagonally, or even backward.

never sacrifice Megan save
safety SOS grateful
Titanic lifeboat Frank secret
stowaways
survivors hero
forget Sean

S	T	O	W	A	W	A	Y	S	T	O
S	A	F	E	T	Y	Y	O	G	I	S
W	O	C	O	M	E	G	A	N	T	U
G	H	E	R	O	T	R	D	E	A	R
R	F	W	Y	I	N	O	T	V	N	V
A	O	K	O	M	F	O	E	E	I	I
T	R	N	A	E	S	I	R	R	C	V
E	G	A	S	M	O	Q	C	O	T	O
F	E	R	A	P	S	O	E	E	N	R
U	T	F	V	L	U	O	S	L	T	S
L	I	F	E	B	O	A	T	O	B	F

GEORGE H. DEAN.
LOST ON
S.S. "TITANIC"
APRIL 15, 1912
AGED 19 YEARS
VERY DEEPLY MOURNED
BY HIS SORROWING PARENTS
FRED & MARY DEAN

News of the disaster reached New York City on the morning of April 15, but the full story became known only when the survivors arrived three days later.

WHY THE SHIP SANK

WHY THE TITANIC SANK

 The gash in the ship's side flooded not just one but a number of the watertight compartments in the hull. That was something that the ship's designers had not planned for. Water spilled over the bulkheads from one compartment to another. As the front of the ship sank deeper, the stern lifted out of the water, placing huge stress on the hull. Eventually, the hull snapped under the weight, and the ship broke in two.

Recent analysis of the wreck of the Titanic suggests that poor quality iron rivets may have snapped.

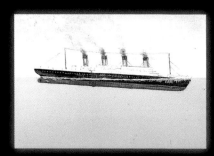
Water pours into the watertight compartments, pulling the bow (front end) down.

As the stern (rear end) rises, stress snaps the main hull. The front part of the ship sinks, pulling the stern with it.

The ship breaks in two. The bow sinks, followed moments later by the stern.

RESCUE

The *Carpathia* arrived at the scene of the sinking at about 4:00 A.M. and spent four hours picking up survivors. Once onboard, they were given blankets and hot drinks. Many were so shocked by their experience that they could not even speak. They arrived in New York three days later.

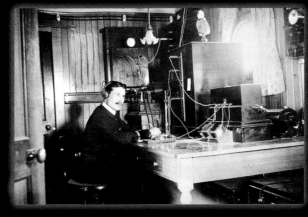

The *Californian's* radio was turned off overnight, so the *Titanic's* distress signal was not heard.

 ## THE SILENT RADIO

The closest ship to the *Titanic* was only two hours away, near enough to reach the liner in time to save many lives. But the *Californian* had turned off its radio. One reason was that the *Titanic's* radio room had sent a rude response earlier, when the *Californian's* warnings about icebergs had interrupted messages they were sending for first-class passengers.

REASONS FOR THE DISASTER

 • NOT ENOUGH LIFEBOATS
The number of lifeboats had been cut to allow more room on deck. The lifeboats could carry a total of 1,178 people—but there were 2,223 people onboard.

 • HIGH SPEED
Some people think that Captain Smith was under pressure from his boss, J. Bruce Ismay, to sail too fast in an area containing icebergs.

 • BINOCULARS
The lookouts' binoculars were locked away. No one knew where the key was.

 • RADIO FAILURE
The ship closest to the *Titanic* had its radio turned off, so the distress calls did not get through.

 • FLAWED DESIGN
The compartments in the hull flooded. Poor-quality rivets might have snapped in the freezing water.

 • CONFUSION
There had been no lifeboat drill—so, in the confusion, the lifeboats were launched with only 712 passengers in them.

 • WEATHER CONDITIONS
Although the sea was calm, there was no moonlight and visibility was poor.

END OF THE VOYAGE

Unlike the *Titanic*, we had made it safely to New York City. The memorial voyage was over —but I was still frustrated about my story. I knew that Frank had died, but what about his two mysterious companions?

As I walked onto the dockside, I saw a man and a woman waiting. They held a bunch of red and yellow flowers. They waved at me, so I went over to speak to them. "Where did you get that suitcase?" asked the man. I told him about finding it in Liverpool and about the two children. The woman smiled and gave me the flowers. "I think these must be for you," she said.

I did not understand. Then the man said, "That suitcase belonged to our grandmother. She and her brother were onboard the *Titanic* as stowaways! That is why we are here, to remember their miraculous survival. And to welcome a new member of the family."

I was confused. The children had made it to New York City safely. But who were they? And what had become of them?

REMEMBRANCE

The woman said, "The children made new lives for themselves in America. But they always felt that they had lost their family . . . first their parents and then their brother. They were always determined to bring their family back together. Now, finally, perhaps they have."

I realized that the couple might be a distant part of my family—perhaps Frank McDowell was a common relative of ours. In any case, they were my only living link to Frank.

ESCAPE TO AMERICA
The woman explained that the children had been wrongly blamed for causing their parents' deaths. They could have gone to prison. But their brother Frank believed in their innocence. He decided to smuggle them onto his next job—as an engineer on the *Titanic*.

 CODE SEVENTEEN: NEW EVIDENCE

The envelope held many tiny pieces that looked as if they had been cut out from newspapers. I had seen something like it before, at the start of my voyage. Can you put the words together to figure out two headlines about the children's story?

parents' | GUILTY | NEW

an | NOT | EVIDENCE

CHILDREN | accident

deaths | SHOWS

CODE EIGHTEEN: WHO WERE THE CHILDREN?

Let's look at the clues . . .

- Their clothes were very old-fashioned.
- Their suitcase contained papers that must have come from onboard the *Titanic*.
- They mysteriously appeared at key places in the *Titanic* story.
- I couldn't find them on my memorial ship.
- They left flowers for Frank McDowell.

LAND OF LIBERTY

For millions of immigrants in the early 20th century, the Statue of Liberty in New York Harbor was a symbol of hope. They thought that the United States would give them an opportunity to work hard and become prosperous. The couple on the dockside told me that both of the children had grown up to have successful careers and happy families.

HEROIC SACRIFICE

The woman said everyone in the American part of the family knew Frank's story. He had carried the children from the storeroom to the deck. He had put them into a lifeboat with a small suitcase. Then he bravely stepped back to try to save others. That was the last time the children saw him.

The couple explained that the children had changed their names on the voyage to keep their identity secret. Sean had changed his name to Leon, and Megan had become Susan. They kept the same last name, though, in honor of their brother: McDowell. I was very pleased to hear that . . . Because there's something I haven't told you yet . . . My full name is Brendan McDowell.

INDEX

PICTURE CREDITS

The Publisher would like to thank the following for permission to reproduce their material. Every care has been taken to trace copyright holders. However, if there have been any unintentional omissions or failure to trace copyright holders, we apologize and will, if informed, endeavor to make corrections in any future edition.

(t = top, b = bottom, c = center, l = left, r = right):

Front and back cover: artwork by Brown Bear Books Ltd.

Pages 6bl and 6cr Topfoto; 6bc Topfoto: Roger-Viollet; 7cl istockphoto; 7tl Alamy: Peter Jordan; 7c Topfoto: The Granger Collection; 7tr Topfoto: Ullstein; 7br Topfoto: The Granger Collection; 8t Getty Images: Science and Society Picture Library; 8c Corbis; 8b Shutterstock; 9tl Topfoto: Ullstein; 9cr Topfoto; 9tc and 9tr Topfoto: Roger-Viollet; 9bl Topfoto: The Granger Collection; 9br Mary Evans Picture Library; 12bl Corbis: Ma Jianguo/Xinhua Press; 12br Picture Nation; 13r Shutterstock; 14c Topfoto: World History Archive; 14b Corbis: Hulton Archive; 15t Ulster Folk & Transport Museum: Harland and Wolff Collection; 15b Topfoto: The Granger Collection; 19t Getty Images: DEAPL; 22bc Shutterstock; 23tl Thinkstock: Photos.com; 23bl istockphoto; 24bl Corbis; 24cl Thinkstock: 24cr Corbis: Ralph White; 24tr, 24cr and 24br Ulster Folk & Transport Museum: Harland & Wolff Collection; 25tl Onslow Auctions Ltd.; 25tr Corbis: Bettmann; 25bl Corbis: Underwood & Underwood; 25br The Father FM Browne S.J. Collection/Irish Picture Library; 28–29b Corbis: Bettmann; 29tr Getty Images: Michel Boutefeu; 29bc Corbis: Ma Jianguo/Xinhua Press; 32l Shutterstock; 32b Thinkstock; 32r Topfoto: Roger-Viollet; 33tl Corbis: Bettmann; 33tc Corbis: Andy Rain; 33tr Topfoto; 33bl Topfoto; 33br Corbis: Sygma; 34br Topfoto: HIP; 34–35 Topfoto: The Granger Collection; 35r Mary Evans Picture Library; 38bl Corbis: Jan Butchofsky; 38bl Alamy; 38bl Thinkstock; 39bl Corbis: Gerry Penny; 39br Alamy: PCL; 40bl Topfoto; 40c Topfoto: Ullstein; 41tl Topfoto; 41tr Topfoto: Roger-Viollet; 45 Shutterstock; 46–47b Corbis: Bettmann; 48br Thinkstock.

The images on pages 7clb, 7blu, 7bl, 7cr, 14b, and 29tc are public domain.

All background images are provided by Shutterstock.

Brown Bear Books Ltd. has made every attempt to contact the copyright holders of all images. If anyone has any updated information relating to image rights, please contact smortimer@windmillbooks.co.uk.

THE SEARCH FOR THE LOST FUGITIVES

This page reveals the answers to all the codes and puzzles. It also explains
how to set the compass in case the directions had you stumped.

THE SOLUTIONS

THE ANSWERS TO THE CODES:

• **CODE ONE** (page 12) The two
headlines are "PARENTS LOSE THEIR
LIVES IN TRAGEDY" and "ORPHANS ARE
BLAMED FOR THE DEATHS."

• **CODE TWO** (page 13) The answers to
the questions that help you figure out
the codes are "Paris," "Belfast," "New
York," and "Smith." The code answers
are "Sean," "Megan," "stowaways,"
"engine room," and "storeroom."

• **CODE THREE** (page 13) The compass
direction from Liverpool to Belfast is
northwest (NW). The message reads:
"Take [the] children [to a] new life."

• **CODE FOUR** (page 18) The scratched
messages read: "What about the rivets?"
"Are there enough lifeboats?"

• **CODE FIVE** (page 18) The compass
direction from Belfast to Southampton
is southeast (SE). The message reads:
"Danger. Do not sail."

• **CODE EIGHT** (page 23) The Morse
code message reads: "The cargo is
safely hidden. FMcD."

• **CODE NINE** (page 28) The compass
direction from Cherbourg to

Queenstown is northwest (NW).
The message reads: "Prove [the]
children innocent."

• **CODE TEN** (page 29) The letters
circled on the first card spell out
"Sean" and "Megan"; the letters on
the second card spell out "Leon"
and "Susan."

• **CODE TWELVE** (page 34) The
message on the card reads: "Our
beloved brother died to save us."

• **CODE THIRTEEN** (page 35) The
Morse Code reads: "The kids are safe."

• **CODE FOURTEEN** (page 35) The
message from the *Titanic* to the
Carpathia (MPA) reads: "Yes come
quick." The message from the
Frankfurt (DFT) to the *Titanic* (MGY)
reads: "Whats the matter with U?"

• **CODE FIFTEEN** (page 38) The
compass direction from Queenstown
to New York City is west-northwest
(WNW). The message reads: "(The) final
clue (is at the) final destination."

• **CODE SEVENTEEN** (page 44) The
headlines read: "NEW EVIDENCE SHOWS
CHILDREN NOT GUILTY" and "PARENTS'
DEATHS AN ACCIDENT."

• **CODE EIGHTEEN** (page 45) The
children must have had a link with the
Titanic and with Frank McDowell. Their
clothes were old-fashioned, as if they
were from the past. They seemed to
appear and disappear . . . almost like
ghosts. The best explanation is that
they must have been Sean and Megan,
the stowaways from the *Titanic*'s voyage.

THE MAZES AND PUZZLES:

• **CODE SIX** (page 19) The entrance
that leads to the storeroom is D.

• **CODE SEVEN** (page 22) Here (below,
right) are the nine differences that show
that the right-hand ticket is a fake.

• **CODE ELEVEN** (page 29) The key
matches the door of the storeroom.

• **CODE SIXTEEN** (page 39) See
above right for the solutions to the
word finder.